Marguerite Bouvet, Helen Maitland Armstrong

Prince Tip-Top

A Fairytale

Marguerite Bouvet, Helen Maitland Armstrong

Prince Tip-Top
A Fairytale

ISBN/EAN: 9783743350618

Manufactured in Europe, USA, Canada, Australia, Japa

Cover: Foto ©Andreas Hilbeck / pixelio.de

Manufactured and distributed by brebook publishing software
(www.brebook.com)

Marguerite Bouvet, Helen Maitland Armstrong

Prince Tip-Top

PRINCE TIP-TOP

A Fairy Tale

BY

MARGUERITE BOUVET

AUTHOR OF "SWEET WILLIAM," "LITTLE MARJORIE'S
LOVE-STORY," ETC., ETC.

Illustrated by

HELEN MAITLAND ARMSTRONG

CHICAGO
A. C. McCLURG AND COMPANY
1892

PRINCE TIP-TOP, FOLLOWED BY PRINCESS CERULEA.
ENTERS THE COUNCIL CHAMBER.

PRINCE TIP-TOP

A Fairy Tale

by

MARGUERITE BOUVET

With illustrations by
Helen Maitland Armstrong

Published at Chicago
by
A·C·McCLURG AND Co.

M·D·CCCXCII

But this Isle,
The greatest and the best of all the main,
He quarters to his blue-hair'd deities.

MILTON.

CONTENTS.

LIST OF ILLUSTRATIONS.

PRINCE TIP-TOP.

I.

PRINCESS CERULEA.

N the days of Nobody-knows-when, and in the land of Nobody-knows-where, there was once a queer little island called Okushee, or the Land of the Cerulites. It is a little singular that a place at once so curious and so attractive should be so entirely unknown to many well-informed people. Few persons have ever visited Okushee, and, to be strictly truthful, I have never met any one who had actually been there, nor could I give you its exact situation on the map. But I should not be at all surprised if it were away out in the middle of one of those vast blue oceans somewhere near the equator, where the sun shines pleasantly, and where the hills are always green, and where the roses bloom the year round, and where the people do little but eat and sleep, and care for nothing but frolic and fun.

The island of Okushee was, I am sure, just such a place as this, and I am sure, too, that it was in many respects a most remarkable country, and that the people who lived in it were perhaps the most remarkable people on the face of the globe. They had strange customs and strange habits and strange laws. They were strictly what might be called an " out-of-the-way " nation, so out of the

way, indeed, that it proved a difficult
task for me to find them at all. They
looked as nobody ever did look or
would ever care to look in one's right
mind, and the most striking thing about
them was their hair. If you will believe
me, these curious creatures were all, for
some unaccountable reason, born with
blue hair, and that is why they were
called Cerulites. Now, a person with
blue hair is a sight not to be met with
every day. You have all heard, I dare
say, the most delightfully absurd stories
about a personage who was so distinguished as to possess a blue beard; but
a whole nation with blue hair is, indeed,
a thing to be wondered at.

Nevertheless, these little people were
very proud of their hair; for the bluer
a person's hair was, the prettier he or
she was supposed to be, and the more
aristocratic. They entertained the pleasing idea that blue hair was a positive

indication of blue blood. Hence, the
kings and queens and all the members
of the royal family had for generations
past been born with the most irre-
proachable blue locks, of all shades and
varieties of that color, from sky-blue
to indigo; and one can scarcely imagine
what a winsome and alluring aspect
they presented.

As might well be expected of people
with such an unheard-of peculiarity,
their ideas and notions were totally
different from those of anybody else.
In the first place, they were blissfully
and supremely ignorant, — which fact
naturally led them to suppose that
they knew everything; and the consequence was that they were the most
self-satisfied, self-complacent set of people to be found anywhere. In contra-
diction to the dismal hue of their
hair, the inhabitants of Okushee were
anything but "blue" in disposition.

They were always cheerful and happy.
In fact, it was considered a great crime
to be unhappy; and those who were in
any way afflicted or distressed were
promptly drowned, that they might not
disturb the peace and contentment of
the rest of the community. To be sure,
they seldom had anything to make
them miserable, for, as I have said, the
island of Okushee was a pleasant place,
where the most delicious fruits grew in
abundance; where no one had to work
to get a living, but lived from day to
day like the careless butterflies of the
fields; where children were never made
to go to school; where boys went swim-
ming and fishing whenever they liked,
and played all sorts of amusing games;
where little girls had picnics every day,
and had the most beautiful clothes for
their dolls, and ate all the chocolate-
creams they wanted. So you can easily
imagine what a heavenly state of things

reigned, and how like a perfect fairy land this little island seemed.

Another very pleasant thing about the Cerulites was that they were all young; and that is why, I think, they never thought of anything but of enjoying themselves. The king and queen were barely in their teens; the chancellor of the exchequer was a mere stripling, and a heedless, hare-brained one at that; and the lord high chamberlain and the keeper of the great seal wore the most disgracefully youthful-looking knickerbockers. All the great dignitaries of the land went right in for a good time just like the rest. Nobody was too wise, or too great, or too important to indulge in the fashionable sports of the season. The consequence was that there was scarcely a day but, had you happened to be in Okushee, you might have seen everybody out in gay holiday attire, frolicking and skylarking about in a way that would certainly have shocked any well-regulated kingdom.

Yet there was one thing, just one thing, that kept the people of this wonderful island from being supremely happy.

Away back in the legendary days of Okushee there had been a royal personage who had so far forgotten his royal manners and his Cerulean ancestry as to fall in love with and marry a chimney-sweep's daughter. This was a serious indiscretion, and one to be punished in no trifling way. The Avenging Fairy of the island forthwith issued a terrible decree. She vowed that at some future time this thoughtless young king and all his noble line should be disgraced by a descendant with black hair. There was a general panic, as you may well suppose, that threatened to overthrow all the Cerulitic doctrines of perpetual

happiness, until at last the Merciful
Fairy, who, you know, is noted for her
happy compromises, stepped in just at
the right minute, and declared that she
would provide some means whereby the
unoffending little heir might be par-
doned, and his baby locks restored to
the approved shade.

But the difficulty was that this means
was to be found only in the most hidden
and mysterious recesses of the Rainbow
Valley. And the little Cerulites said
they were blessed if they knew *where*
the Rainbow Valley was. Nobody
knew anything about it, nobody had
ever heard of it, and only the most
diligent and persistent search would
ever find it; and as they abhorred and
detested nothing so much as exerting
themselves, the Rainbow Valley had
not yet been discovered, and the Cerulites were still living with this terrible
calamity hanging over them. Time

went on, and one generation succeeded
another, and as regularly as a little heir
to the throne was expected, there was
secret consternation in the hearts of
the royal couple, and, indeed, of all
their subjects; and as regularly, too, a
great reward, sometimes in the shape of
a bag of treasures, sometimes in the
shape of a beautiful young princess,
was offered to the person who would go
and find the mystic Rainbow Valley.
Then, of course, for nearly a week everybody went about with a great show of
enthusiasm, which, however, soon subsided into the usual easy-going way.
And when the little heir of Okushee
appeared, and he was found to bear no
mark of disgrace on his small scalp,
these gay, light-hearted little people
went their way rejoicing, and troubled
themselves no more about the good
fairy's promise.   But the custom of
dreading the birth of a new child in the

royal family, and of offering the enti-
cing reward for the discovery of the
Rainbow Valley, had grown to be a
regular institution, which never failed to
be ceremoniously observed.

It so happened that the present king
and queen of Okushee had a little
daughter born to them, the sweetest,
dearest, most winsome baby-girl — according to Cerulitic notions — that ever
blessed two fond parents. In the first
place, she came into the world with a
quantity of pale-blue ringlets, — just that
delicate, tender hue which we see in the
summer heavens. Her eyes were of a
deep azure, and her cheeks were pink
and white. Then, too, strictly in ac-
cordance with the moral code, she was
the brightest, happiest, most amiable
baby in the world. She was never
known to cry once, not through all her
babyhood, which lasted nearly six weeks.
Before she was a year old she could

"The most winsome baby-girl that ever blessed two
fond parents."

sing like a lark and discuss politics in a
way that shamed every statesman in
the kingdom. The day after she was
born she had cut all her teeth, — white,
cunning little teeth that shone like a
row of pearls when she smiled. This
was considered a most favorable omen,
and one which signified that her reign
would be a singularly prosperous and
happy one.

The most learned philosophers of the
kingdom came to pay their respects to
her, and to look at her, and to pass
their judgment on this small phenome-
non, and they all agreed — which is a
strange enough thing for learned men
to do — that she was the most remarkable child ever born in the island of
Okushee, and the royal couple were
overwhelmed with joy. After a long
and animated session in the chamber of
parliament, it was decided that she
should be named Cerulea, on account

of the ravishing hue of her hair; and
Princess Cerulea she was from that day
forth.

If I were to tell you all the things
that this little princess had to make her
happy and comfortable, I greatly fear
that you might become discontented
with your own fortunes in this world,
and perhaps be a little envious of her
blessings.   But the life of a child like"
Princess Cerulea can scarcely be imag-
ined by any one who has not been
fortunate enough to be born in the
royal house of Okushee.   She was the
idol of doting parents and, indeed, of a
whole nation.   Not a day passed but
some festivities were held in her honor.
The rarest gifts and the costliest treasures were brought to her from all
parts of the kingdom, and nothing
was thought too good for her.   And
although her education was in some
ways sadly neglected, and she might

have been considered elsewhere a most
ignorant young person, yet her advice
was sought on all important matters of
state, and her wishes consulted in everything.

But, like many of the good things of
this world, this happy period of maiden-
hood, though sweet, was short.   For
among the many simple notions of
the Cerulites, was that of very early
marriages.   Young women who were at
all eligible were married and settled at
the tender age of eight.   A young person of ten was deemed quite *passée*, and
at twelve she was a hopeless old maid.
So it was not long before the royal
couple began to think of finding a suit-
able husband for their daughter Cerulea.
One day, when the king and queen
were sitting cosily on their thrones, all
dressed up in their royal robes and
jewelled crowns, and looking very fine
indeed, the king turned to his wife, and

putting his spectacles on his nose, said, with a knowing air, —

"My dear, is n't it about time we had a wedding? In less than a month our daughter will have reached the mature age of seven, and we really ought to be looking around us for a — for a —"

"Prince?" suggested the queen.

"For a husband of some sort, unless we want her on our hands for the rest of our natural life."

"What!" screamed the queen, with much maternal indignation, "a husband of some sort! Why, how your Majesty does talk! Cerulea had twenty-six offers last week, and seventeen the week before; and she might —"

"Well, well, don't let our words ruffle your sweet temper," returned the king, majestically. "Our royal consent is granted, and she may accept one of them, at least."

The queen turned and gazed at her loving consort with a look of wild surprise.

"Sire!" said she, "can it be that you are committing the folly of supposing that any nobleman in Okushee is worthy of Cerulea's hand? Think for one moment; compare *their* hair to hers, and then answer me."

"We were not committing the folly of supposing anything of the kind," rejoined the young monarch, with a sudden cough to hide his embarrassment, for her last appeal was unanswerable, and he knew it; "but — but —"

"Then what *was* your Gracious Majesty supposing?" interrupted the queen, vehemently.

"I was only thinking that it is high time Cerulea was married, if she is ever going to be," responded the king, suddenly, forgetting his kingly phrases; "and you and she may attend to it.

I wash my hands of the whole business ! "

Now this was just what the queen expected and wanted most, — to have the whole matter in her own hands; for she and Cerulea had discussed the subject before, and were about of the same mind. So she looked up at her lord, and smiling sweetly, said, —

" Ah, my liege, now you speak like a king and a Cerulite. I, too, have been pondering over this serious matter. But it is plain that the Princess Cerulea cannot possibly marry any noble youth in Okushee, for there is not among them a single one with just the royal shade of hair."

The king put his forefinger to his chin, and mused for some time over this obstacle. Then he took his wife's hand affectionately, and said, " My love, have you not — a — could you not — with your usual cleverness

and ingenuity — suggest — a — a way
out of this?"

"Since your Majesty is so gracious,"
said the queen, with a modest courtesy,
"I think I can, if your Majesty will be
so good as to listen to me."

"We are all attention," replied the
king, eagerly; and he bent his lordly
ear and wrinkled his lordly brow in
quite an earnest way.

"Your Majesty has perhaps heard the
wise Pollyphrastus, our most estimable
councillor, say that there are many
countries beyond Okushee, where kings
and great and worthy princes abound.
There is even, he says, a new country
across the waters, a country but lately
discovered, called America, which
might, perhaps, offer a prince to Cerulea's liking. Now, we will send out
heralds to all these distant lands, and
have them proclaim the charms and
graces of our daughter the princess,

3

and invite a score of royal personages
to attend Cerulea's birthday ball.   It
is likely enough that among them there
will be at least one princely youth
deserving of Cerulea's hand and of your
royal favor."

"A great and wise idea! An un-
commonly great and wise idea!" exclaimed the young king, with enthusiasm, and he gave his knee a sounding
slap to express his immense satisfaction.
"It shall be done at once!" and then
he added, with a confidential air, "We
had been thinking of the very same
thing ourself, my dear, we had indeed!"

Now, the queen had certain doubts
about this, but she kept them to herself,
like a prudent, politic little queen that
she was.   And then the royal couple
embraced each other lovingly, and the
queen went off to tell Cerulea the
happy news, and to make preparations
for the ball, while her liege summoned

The queen suggests a way out of the difficulty.

his chief advisers for a rousing good
game of tiddledywinks.

It was not many days before the
whole island was alive with interest in
the coming festivities. For a birthday
ball was, to the Cerulites, the promise
of all manner of merry-making. Every
one talked about it, every one conjec-
tured on the probable fortunes of the
fair Cerulea, and every one was delighted
with the unique idea of inviting strange
princes to sue for the hand of the princess. Such a thing had never been
heard of before! The little scullions
in the king's kitchen seemed greatly
amused at the idea, and giggled over it
as only kitchen scullions can; and the
cooks opened their mouths very wide,
and crossed their hands on their broad
white aprons, and said, " It was jest like
Miss Ceruly's noble ma!"

In the course of time a dozen spright-
ly young heralds, splendidly gotten up in

red and black suits, wearing cocked
hats and blowing long trumpets, set
out, according to the queen's wishes, to
all the nations they had ever heard of;
and they took with them such glowing
accounts of their young princess, of her
beauty and virtues and learning, and
chiefly of the marvellous color of her
hair, which they said was the joy of the
royal family and the envy of · all the
other noble ladies of Okushee, that very
soon all the eager kings and queens
were wild to have their sons try their
fortune. And as it was also rumored
that she was very rich, and that she
would inherit the whole of that wonderful island called Okushee, the fair
Cerulea was considered an exceedingly
desirable daughter-in-law.

Consequently, a little more than a
fortnight after, these dutiful heralds
returned with a regular procession of
youthful suitors from nearly every polite

nation in the world. They arrived on
the very night of Cerulea's birthday
ball, and of course the greatest excitement prevailed, since the young princes
were to be received with much *éclat*, as
became their exalted station. There
were torch-lights, red, yellow, and green,
illuminating every road which led up to
the king's palace. The gardens and
lawns were festooned with flowers and
Chinese lanterns, and every window of
the great white marble palace was aglow
with pink and blue lights. There was a
magnificent display of fireworks too, —
Roman candles, and " wheels " without
end, and sky-rockets shooting up in-
cessantly. The king's picked orches-
tra played the loveliest, dreamiest dance-
music, and the white fountains spouted
and tossed their jets in the moonlight,
and added their noise and light to this
enchanted scene, while the distant stars
looked down upon it all, and seemed to

smile pleasantly because these little
people were having such a glorious
good time.

Of course the young Cerulite ladies
looked perfectly lovely in their gauzy
dresses, and bewitching little pink bows
in their hair. And the young gentlemen seemed the picture of contentment
as they bent over their fair companions
and airily discussed the great topic of
the day.

"Dear me!" said one fair damsel to
the young gallant at her side, "was n't
that a famous idea, to invite a lot of
strange creatures to the princess's ball?
One would think there were no charming gentlemen on the island," she added,
with an arch smile.

"One would, indeed," assented the
flattered youth. "But *you* think there
are, now don't you?"

"Oh, do I?" laughed the fair Cerulite,
and her eyebrows went up inquiringly.

"Of course you do. But I wish
those noble young persons would come.
Don't you wonder what they will be
like?"

"Well, rather," smiled the little lady,
and she shrugged her pretty shoulders
and tossed her saucy head in a way that
ravished her companion.

"I really hope their hair will be blue
enough to suit her Majesty's notion,"
said the young gentleman, sardonically.

"So do I; but she *is* very particular,
they say, and I don't blame her; for
there is no denying it, her own hair is
the most gorgeous shade I ever saw!
But see, there she is now!"

Sure enough, Princess Cerulea had
just stepped into the brilliant garden,
accompanied by her royal mamma, and
followed by her maid Pattidan. She
seated herself on a little divan made of
daisies and violets, where throngs of
admirers came to pay their homage and

congratulations to her. Indeed, she was sweet and ravishing in her soft, silvery gown, with her waves of pale blue hair cascading down her white arms and shoulders. She smiled and bowed graciously to every one, and swayed her ostrich fan in the most fashionable manner, and cast such languid glances at her young courtiers that their gallant hearts began to thump very loudly, and the other young ladies were more envious than ever. But it was quite plain to be seen that in spite of all her pretty wiles and graces, she was in a dreadful state of expectancy. The foreign suitors had not yet made their appearance, and she was suffering for a sight of them. The dancing had begun; the ladies and gentlemen were flitting about on the lawn like bright butterflies underneath the colored lights: some were walking arm in arm in the more dreamy rays of the moon, and talking together in lover-like fashion, while others sat apart in little groups, gossiping and flirting in the most conventional manner; but all were, like Cerulea, eagerly awaiting the great event.

At last the majestic horns of the heralds were heard in the distance, and shouts of " Here they come! Make way for the cavalcade!" resounded on every side. Such shouting and pushing, and waving of banners, and general excitement as there was!

It was simply bewildering. Everybody rushed to the front to behold the new-comers. The king and queen, quite forgetting their royal dignity, came running down the palace steps with the rest. The estimable Pollyphrastus, in his hurry, tripped his foot in his Oxford gown, and fell flat upon his learned nose, and the princess was in a state of agitation not easily depicted. All the festivities and merry-makings were suspended for the time, and everything else was forgotten. For it was in truth the young suitors, a whole regiment of them, advancing, with great trumpery and clashing of cymbals, and a prodigious amount of noise and glitter. Each one was mounted on a pretty little pony, such as only the Cerulites have, and each was decked out according to his notion of what was befitting an occasion like this; and you may believe that together they presented a most unique and grotesque appearance. They made a beautiful procession, such as the little Cerulites had never dreamed of. They marched up slowly and in great state towards the palace, the heralds following on foot and carrying the national flags of each, while the band played all the way.

But as the suitors rode through the open ranks, smiling, and doffing their

caps right and left, the expectant little
Cerulites were suddenly stricken dumb
with horror! As you have no doubt
guessed, not one of these civilized and
high-born princes was gifted with blue
hair! There were black, and brown,
and yellow curly heads, — indeed, heads
of every sensible color except the approved and much-sought blue; and
the inhabitants of Okushee looked on
aghast, with woe and dismay written on
their countenances. Many of the ladies
went straight into hysterics; the queen
fainted dead away, and came to only
after prolonged pokings and pinchings
from her maids of honor; and the disappointed and mortified spectators
uttered little shrieks that were quite
heart-rending. There was a general
stampede, of course, and grief and con-
fusion reigned supreme. The young
king had a sad time restoring order,
which he did, however, after some effort.

With great presence of mind, he called
for soda-water and smelling-bottles.
Princess Cerulea exhibited more com-
posure and dignity than the other
ladies, but she looked very pale and
weak, and Pattidan was obliged to fan
her vigorously, and to administer the
vinaigrette more than once during the
evening.

But, as you already know, the Cerulites could not long remain in this
condition of moral depression, and
what with ices and smelling-salts and
other aids to comfort, they very soon
recovered from this severe shock to
their nerves, and their spirits rose
to a corresponding pitch. And when
they discovered what really great and
interesting personages they had invited
to their island, they willingly over-
looked that slight defect in the matter
of hair.

While the Cerulites are enjoying this

more comfortable frame of mind, and
becoming acquainted with their strange
guests, I will give you a little account

The young princes are presented to the royal couple.

of some of the more prominent figures
in this startling array of young suitors,
as each one alighted from his little
pony, and was ceremoniously presented
to the royal couple and their royal
daughter.

II

PRINCE TIP-TOP.

IRST of all there came a little fat Dutchman, a jolly little prince of the illustrious house of Roth-nase, whose an-cestors were all famous for the beautiful bloom on their noses, and likewise for their fondness for beer. This little fellow was a worthy representative of his noble line; and when he was offered a goblet of foaming soda, mis-taking it for his favorite beverage, he

4

plunged into it so eagerly that he
sneezed and choked in a way that made
everybody laugh.

Next came a little Frenchman, a thin,
wiry, black-eyed young Bourbon, who
" had no love for Napoleon," and who
gave himself a thousand airs, and yet
was so astonishingly civil to everybody
that he made a good impression at
first. I shall not attempt to tell you
what *his* feelings were when he found
himself in the company of such very
queer people; because, in the first place,
some of his feelings were indescribable,
and secondly, because, being a little
Frenchman, he was too extremely
polite to show all he felt.

After him came a frowsy-looking
individual, with a bushy wig, dressed
up in the most remarkable fur coat and
cap, and looking for all the world like
a young bear. It was hinted by some
of the courtiers that he came from the

North Pole; but I think he must have been a little Esquimaux of very distinguished parentage; and he was ugly enough to please even the most fastidious taste in Okushee.

Then there was a stout young Briton, a Knight of the Garter, if I am not mistaken, who evidently thought himself of great consequence, and displayed all his grandpapa's orders and ribbons, and who was considered a killing swell at home. He had an alarming appetite too, and turned up his pretty nose irreverently at the delicacies offered him by the Cerulites, and exclaimed loudly, —

"Bless my buttons! Where's the roast-beef and the plum-pudding?"

The next notable was a youthful Turkish pasha, in a gay red turban and very loose trousers, who sported a long pipe, and who turned out to be a desperate flirt.

There was also a young nobleman from Russsia, his Excellency the Chevalier de Skzlawitchgnwski, about whom we shall have little to say, as his name is so very unpleasant.

Another most estimable personage was little Prince Sum-Fun, lately arrived from Ching-a-Lung-lang, a Chinaman of great distinction, whose chief attraction was a long and beautiful pigtail, which trailed behind him in quite a regal way, and which was the wonder and admiration of all beholders. I am sure, if it had only been of a beautiful pale-blue tint, the guileless little Cerulea would have fancied him on the spot.

At the very end of the procession, however, came the last, and by far the most lovable, of all these youthful suitors. This was a little American boy from a very large city, who was duly presented to the royal family as Prince Tip-Top.

About this Prince Tip-Top I shall
have much to say, for he was certainly
the prettiest and dearest little fellow
that ever any Cerulite had seen. And,
as Pattidan well said to her young
mistress that night, after the ball, he
was "as sweet as a pink, and looked as
if he 'd jest stepped out of fairyland."
He had a bright, rosy little face, and
the sweetest smiling mouth in the world,
—a mouth that looked as if it had never
said an unkind or ungentle thing.
And yet he had big dark eyes that
were brimful of wholesome mischief,
and the sauciest of little noses, and the
roundest of little chins, and the loveliest
of shining yellow curls falling all over
his straight shoulders, — all of which
made you fall in love with him before
you had been with him ten minutes.
Then he looked so graceful and courtly
in his silk and velvet clothes and his
dainty, plumed cap that there was not

a more irresistible person on the island
that night, not even Cerulea herself.

Of course all the ladies were charmed,
the princess in particular; and of course
all the gentlemen were madly jealous,
for Prince Tip-Top made himself so
very agreeable, and had such fascina-
ting manners, that the other little noble-
men fairly paled beside him, and some
of them actually turned green with
envy.

He stood by Cerulea's flowered sofa,
airily twirling his cap in his hand, and
talking to everybody at once in his
most engaging manner, while his eyes
danced all the while with excitement.

" Indeed," he said, looking about on
the gay and festive scene, "this is the
grandest show I have ever been to.   I
declare it reminds me of the Fourth of
July."

" Oh, does it?" said the princess, with
a killing look.

"Oh, what is the Fourth of July?
Tell us about it, do, do!" cried a chorus
of ladies' voices.

"Don't you know?" asked Tip-Top,
in some surprise. "Why, I thought
everybody knew about the Fourth of
July. Well, it's our national holiday,
and a jolly day it is, too, for us boys.
It's ever so much like this, only as I'm
thought rather young at home, I have
never been invited to quite such a swell
celebration as this; and I have never
seen so many charming ladies, with — a
— with such — a — such beautiful hair!"
he added, with great gallantry.

The young ladies all laughed, and
admired Tip-Top's yellow curls in an
audible undertone; and some, who were
very kindly disposed, said that blue and
gold were lovely together, and that he
and the princess made not such a bad
looking couple, after all.

"We have all sorts of larks on *our*

Fourth of July," related Tip-Top, with animation. "We have cannon shooting early in the morning, and firecrackers and brass bands all day long, and the grandest fireworks and torch-light processions in the evening. And then big men go about making speeches, and talk about George Washington and the Declaration of Independence; for that is the right thing to do on that day, you know."

"It must be very delightful!" said the ladies, who were really not taking in any of these patriotic facts, but only Tip-Top's bright glances and sweet smiles.

"When I am a —" (he was going to say "when I am a man," but he checked himself, remembering that just now he was supposed to be a full-fledged gentleman, and that he was playing the part of one at least), — "When I am married," he continued, with amazing

Prince Tip-Top captivates the Princess Cerulea.

coolness, "we will invite you *all* to go
to America with us and see for your-
selves, won't we?" and he turned to
the princess and looked at her so that
she blushed rosy red. "And I hope
you will come, and that you will have
as good a time as I am having now."

They thought it would be delightful.
Indeed, anything in which Prince Tip-
Top was concerned would be delightful,
they were sure, and the gentle Cerulea
thought so too.

The king and queen were greatly
impressed by this generous invitation.
They had never before been asked to
visit any other country, they and all
their subjects, and it struck them as
being a pleasing novelty. Tip-Top
immediately won for himself the royal
favor by this stroke of policy. The
king told his wife privately that
"Prince Tip-Top" sounded like a very
noble name, and the queen agreed with

him; whereupon the king put his arm
in Tip-Top's and called him " My dear
fellow," in the most familiar way; and
the queen danced three cotillons with
him, and pronounced him a most
accomplished dancer; and the princess
waltzed with him so many times in
succession that people began to comment upon it.

The fact was that Prince Tip-Top
was " going on in a shocking way," as
his rivals expressed it, — that is, doing
his best to make himself most attractive
to his royal hosts, and succeeding admir-
ably well. So that the exasperated
young gentlemen who had been wall-
flowers most of the evening began to
make remarks upon his audacious behavior, and the confident manner in which
he boasted of marrying the princess,
without so much as " by your leave," to
anybody! But Tip-Top did not mind
his rivals a particle; he was, without

doubt, the lion of the evening, and he knew it, and was enjoying himself hugely. He could not help wishing secretly that his little friends at home might behold him in his triumph. What *would* they say if they could but see him disporting himself in this free and easy way with kings and queens and princesses! What fun it would be to tell them about it when he returned, and to sit back and watch the effect of his astounding news! It was his merry little companions at home who had so aptly nicknamed him Prince Tip-Top, because he was always at the head of all their sports, and was withal so exquisite and pretty and dear, and because they all admired and courted him greatly. But with these foreign princes, whom he was rivalling in the affections of the fair Cerulea, it was very different. They had none too high an opinion of an *American nobleman*, and his popularity and gracious airs were insufferable.

When at last the ball was fairly over, and the festivities broke up at an unusually late hour, Prince Tip-Top took leave of his new friends in a way that was grace itself; and immediately the queen invited him to stay all night at the palace, and offered him her very best and choicest apartments, which he joyfully accepted,— at which crowning insult the less-favored suitors, who were by this time consumed with wrath and indignation, straightway made up their minds to check that young Top-Knot, as they called him. And the little English lord and the young Bourbon proposed to look up his ancestry the very next day, and find out how he came by the title of prince, forsooth! and who his grandfather and great-grandfather were, and very shortly

show him up in all his vulgar lineage
as an upstart and an impostor.

Dear little Prince Tip-Top! How
little did he dream, as he lay that night
in the best bed of the palace, and
thought over the splendid time he had
had, and of all the frolic yet to come,
and wondered which of his pretty suits
he should wear on the morrow, — how
little did he dream, I say, of the unpleasant intentions of his enemies, and
the downfall in store for him! Indeed,
he was too happy to have any such
forebodings. He could think of
nothing but the pretty princess, and
of the king and queen who had been
so kind to him, and who were so young
that they seemed just like his own little
playfellows at home. And then he
tried to think of his family so far away
in America, — so far, indeed, that he
began to doubt whether he ever had
any family at all; and somehow that

charming little Cerulea, with her impossible hair and her bewitching little ways,
was the only image that would stay
before him; and the more he thought
it over, the more convinced he became
that blue hair was not such an extraor-
dinary thing after all. And gradually
all the strange things he had witnessed
had grown so natural and familiar to
him that he felt as if he had never been
anywhere but in Okushee, or known
anybody but these little Cerulites; in
which hazy frame of mind he soon fell
sound asleep on his snowy pillow.

The morning after the party, Princess
Cerulea sat in her boudoir, before the
looking-glass, admiring herself, while
Pattidan arranged her long hair. She
did look unusually pretty that morning,
and Pattidan's tongue was particularly
lively in praising her mistress and telling her all the fine compliments she
had heard from the young gentlemen;

for Pattidan had a way of hearing and knowing everything that was agreeable. But Cerulea was not thinking so much about compliments as she was of a certain little prince with shining yellow curls and brown eyes ; and she did wish that Pattidan would talk about him instead of the others who were not half so pretty, or half so sweet, or half so noble looking. Pattidan knew this very well, the artful hussy, but she would talk right along about everything else, just to plague her little mistress, I suppose.

"I say, now, Miss, that little Chiny lord with the sweet pig-tail, is n't he a beauty, though!"

"Gracious! Pattidan, how can you say so," said her Highness, with a look of intense disgust. "Why, I never saw anything so ridiculous as that queue. I never could abide a queue, any way, — you know that very well."

"La, Miss! and was n't it yourself as said his Majesty, the Prince Sum-Fun, was a likely young man enough, and would n't be at all bad-looking if it was n't that his queue is black instead of blue, like your own sweet ringlets," said the wily Pattidan, patting and stroking the ringlets in question affectionately.

"Oh, well, that was before I had seen them *all*, Pattidan; I had n't seen everybody when I said that."

"Well, there is a whole regiment of 'em, I allow, and I don't see, for my part, how your sweet ladyship is ever going to make up your mind amongst so many."

"Ha, ha, ha!" laughed Cerulea, "that is easy enough, my dear; for to tell you the truth, I have seen only one that I think is a really, truly prince!"

"And which one 's that?" asked Pattidan, feigning to be eaten up with curiosity.

"Why, bless your stupidity, Pattidan, can't you see?"

"Lor! Miss, I am dretful stoopid, but maybe I can guess. It's the young Turkey-gobbler, with the red silk night-cap and the blue silk pantaloons," suggested Pattidan.

"No, it is not the Pasha of Turkey," returned Cerulea, emphatically.

"Then it's that wigglesome little French Bon-bon."

"Pattidan! I'm surprised at you, I really am. Give yourself the trouble to look at his hair by daylight, and then ask yourself if I could submit to the agonizing mortification of such an alliance."

"His hair is 'most as black as a crow's feathers, indeed it is, your Worship; and that's a bad sign, a powerful bad sign."

"I should think it was," said Cerulea, warmly,—"it is a sign one has no royal blood in one's veins."

"My good gracious, Miss, you don't
tell me!" ejaculated Pattidan, who was
pardonably ignorant on points of social
distinction.

"Of course I do;" and the little
princess admired her own heavenly
tresses, with an air of happy superiority
which she rarely indulged in, for she
was not, as a rule, vain of her great
attraction.

"But, your Highness, you don't
mean to say that all them fine dooks
and princes is n't royal born," inquired
Pattidan, in a horrified tone, "and that
you 're going to marry one of 'em,
anyhow?"

"No, Pattidan, I am not going to
marry any one who has not the bluest
and royallest blood in his veins," replied
the princess, with a determined shake
of her head; and she little thought that
she should soon have cause to rue these
rash words. "So you need not be

" No, Pattidan, I am not going to marry any one who has not the bluest and
royallest blood in his veins ! "

alarmed. And as for marrying a person with black hair, why that is the height of impropriety."

"Then, Miss, what's your majestic pa going to do with all them gay birds, in their Sunday feathers; they're every one of them just wild about you, Miss."

"I really don't know," said Cerulea, seeming greatly perplexed. "We shall have to consult the wise Pollyphrastus. But it is a great disappointment to find all these young persons with such absurd hair."

"That it is, your Majesty, and I dare say it'll be a great disappointment to them, the poor young gentlemen. I feel for 'em, I do, especially for that sweet little young prince from Ameriky, Prince Top-Knot, is it?"

"Prince Tip-Top," corrected Cerulea.

"For my part, Miss, I never see anything so aristocratic and sort of elegant-like as those legs of his; and he does look so bewitched with you, Miss."

Here Princess Cerulea brightened up astonishingly, and laughed a coy little laugh, and said, in her most coquettish manner, —

"Get along with you, Pattidan; how can he be bewitched with me when he has seen me just once."

"Indeed, that's quite enough, bless your sweet ladyship," replied the loyal and devoted handmaid. "It's quite enough, as any of those young dooks will tell you."

Princess Cerulea blushed at this compliment in a way that was not in the least unbecoming. If any of her eager lovers could have caught a glimpse of her just at that moment, with that delicate bloom on her cheeks, in dainty contrast to her beautiful blue ripples of hair, they certainly must have adored her frantically, and been in despair about their own vulgar chevelures.

"Now, Pattidan," said the little princess, in a confidential whisper, "I am going to tell you a secret, a very great secret, Pattidan! I am going to tell you what I think about Prince Tip-Top. I think that *he* is the only real prince among them all."

"Just what I've thought all along, Miss; only his hair —"

"Is beautiful," interrupted Cerulea. "Golden hair may be a mark of royalty in America, you know, for gold is a royal color. But I shall go and ask Pollyphrastus this very minute."

"It's a great pity, though, that Pollyphrastus hasn't been bright enough to find the Rainbow Valley, in all these years. Then that dear little Prince Tip-Toe might have as blue a head of

hair as anybody, and there would be
no trouble, and everything would be
lovely."

Cerulea gave a little sigh, and
said it was indeed a great pity.   But
as it would have been deemed highly
presumptuous in her to cast reflections
on the wisdom of the great Pollyphrastus, Cerulea did not pursue the
subject any farther.   Her toilet being
by this time quite completed, she
sallied out into the palace gardens to
take a morning walk before going to
consult the king and his chief adviser
on the weighty subject which now
absorbed her thoughts.

By a singular coincidence, Prince
Tip-Top had also come out for an
early walk, so that almost the first
person Cerulea came upon as she
tripped down the white walk, was a
graceful and gayly attired young man,
who smiled sweetly the minute he saw

By a singular coincidence Prince Tip-Top had also come out
for an early walk.

her, and dropped upon his knee before
her, and kissed her hand in the most
courtly and lover-like fashion.   He was
dressed in a beautiful pale pink velvet
suit, just the color of the rosy morning,
with a satin ruff around his neck, and
satin puffs on his sleeves, and satin
rosettes on his garters, and beautiful
gold buckles on his dainty shoes.   He
wore a neat little hat ornamented with
gold lace and white ostrich-plumes, and
he carried an exquisite bit of a cane in
his hand.

Princess Cerulea stood as though
transfixed when she saw this bewildering pink apparition; she could hardly
speak for emotion.   But Tip-Top, who
was always at his ease, and knew very
well how to make people feel comfortable, began by saying he hoped she
had slept well; and he thanked her
again and again for the delightful time
he had had at her ball the night before,

and said how much he had enjoyed it, and what a pleasant place Okushee was, and wondered why he had never heard of it before. And then he told her all about his home in America, and his little friends there, and his Aunt Jane,— all which seemed greatly to interest the fair Cerulea. So they walked on for nearly an hour, talking as freely as if they had known each other always, and having the best kind of a time. And they were so happy in each other's society that Cerulea quite forgot to go and consult the learned Pollyphrastus on the perplexing question of royalty without blue hair, — indeed she quite forgot that Prince Tip-Top's curls were only golden, so agreeable and attractive did he make himself to her.

But there were those who had not forgotten their suspicions concerning Prince Tip-Top's pretensions to royal lineage,— who believed, in fact, that his claims had slender foundation.

It so happened, therefore, that just as Tip-Top and the pretty princess were walking about the garden hand in hand, whom should they meet but a half-dozen or more of Tip-Top's most formidable rivals, who were holding a very animated consultation. Young Bourbon began to gesticulate fiercely with his wiry little arms and legs when he saw the smiling couple advancing towards them; my lord's countenance assumed a look of withering scorn; the Turkish pasha's wore a savage expression; and Prince Sum-Fun gave way to his feelings by viciously tying hard knots in his pig-tail. They were all consumed with envy. To think that this young nobody— this upstart of the day before yesterday — should get the better of them in this fashion, just because he could look sweet, and dance

well with those pretty legs of his, and
had yellow curls, which should have
been a disgrace to him in a country
where nothing but blue hair was toler-
ated!   It was scandalous!

Of course Tip-Top did not suspect
the thoughts of these evil-minded
young gentlemen, so he smiled, and
greeted them in his kindliest manner.
But nothing could be less cordial than
their behavior towards him.   They
utterly ignored his friendly speeches,
and after paying their respects to the
princess, they excused themselves, saying they had affairs of the greatest
importance to attend to; and with a
look of terrible meaning at Prince Tip-
Top, they departed.

Straightway they went to the king's
council-chamber and laid their suspicions before his Majesty, who, greatly
agitated by the news, immediately
called in his clever-minded queen; who,

declaring that it was too much for her, referred the matter to the learned Polly-phrastus. This gentleman of course was much perturbed; he had by some singular oversight omitted to look into the politics of this new country whence the eligible Tip-Top came, and he now trembled lest he had committed the un-pardonable blunder of admitting into the kingdom a person with no blue blood in his veins, and no blue tinge in his hair.

He tried to dispute this question with the base accusers, and called for proofs regarding Tip-Top's low origin. But these riotous young suitors only shouted with laughter at the very idea.

"Proof! My stars and garters! who ever heard of an American prince?" shouted the little Briton, whose noble grandpapa traced his descent back to William the Conqueror.

"Whoever heard of the royal house

6

of Tip-Top!" roared the Russian with the unpronounceable name.

"Ha, ha, ha!" cried the little Frenchman, and he turned a somersault in his excitement.

"Call the council to order!" thundered the king, in tones of awful severity; and Pollyphrastus pounded on the back of the throne with the great seal.

"Now bring forth the Book of Wisdom, and summon his Highness, the high and mighty Prince Tip-Top, of the royal house of Tip-Top, and let him make his own defence!" commanded the king, with increasing dignity and a magnificent wave of the hand.

The young suitors giggled; whereon the young monarch frowned savagely at them. An attendant hurried out to seek Prince Tip-Top. The anxious Pollyphrastus pulled down the Book of Wisdom from a very high shelf, and fell to turning over its leaves and running his finger up and down its columns, in a way which plainly betrayed his agitation and the importance of the occasion.

In a moment more Prince Tip-Top appeared upon the scene, wondering what had happened, and why he was called up so suddenly, and what this queer meeting was all about, and what he had done to make everybody stare at him so. In his excitement he looked prettier than ever; his brown eyes grew big and inquiring, and his cheeks were like two red poppies: but his face was truthful and honest, and showed that he was an innocent little fellow, whatever was his ancestry. Princess Cerulea had followed him, and she, too, was in an agony of suspense. When she saw the councillor poring over the Book of Wisdom, and observed the wrinkle on her royal papa's brows, and heard muffled whisperings of "im-

postor " and " upstart " and " humbug,"
and saw all eyes directed to Tip-Top's
rosy figure, her worst misgivings were
confirmed.

The king proceeded to business without delay, and called upon Prince Tip-
Top — albeit with great respect and
courtesy — to relate the history of his
descent, to tell the assembly how he
came by the title of Prince Tip-Top,
and, in fine, to state what his claims to
royalty were.

" Well," said Tip-Top, throwing back
his head, " I will!" and he spoke with
the confidence that comes of knowing
one's self in the right; for he had
been very careful to go through all the
branches of his family-tree before start-
ing out on this eventful journey. " In
the first place, I am called Prince
Tip-Top because — because — " he
stammered, with becoming modesty,
" because the boys at home liked me;

and secondly, because I'm descended
from Henry the Eighth of England!"

This statement was received with
deafening applause on the part of the
courtiers who sympathized with Tip-
Top, in which the king and queen and
the princess, and even Pattidan, joined
vociferously.

" How are you descended from Henry
the Eighth?" demanded Pollyphrastus,
with a judicial squint.

Tip-Top pulled a bit of a note-book
from one of his pockets, and opened it
at a certain well-worn page, — only to
get "a start," as it were, for he had it
all by heart, like his catechism, — and
then he began with great stress: —

" My grandmother's great-aunt was a
Jenkins, and *her* grandmother's great-
aunt was a Simmons, and *her* grandmother's great-aunt was a Jones, and *her*
grandmother's great-aunt was a Robin-
son, and *she* married her sister's second

cousin-in-law, and *he* was a Tudor; and the Tudors, as every one knows, are all descended from Henry the Eighth."

Everybody drew a long breath. The king looked enchanted. Pollyphrastus beamed at Tip-Top over his spectacles, and the dismayed rivals began to wilt one by one. Before such a battalion of facts it seemed as if there was really nothing to do but submit.

"Nothing could be more clear and satisfactory," said the king; and he was on the point of shaking hands with Tip-Top and congratulating him, when that suspicious, interfering little Frenchman called out, —

"Nossing could be more foggy or more *un*satisfactory. Look in zee vonderful Book of zee Visdom, and see if it ees correct!"

"Look in das buch!" echoed the fat Dutchman, with owlish glee.

"Look in the Book of Wisdom, by

Prince Tip-Top, followed by Princess Cerulea, enters the Council Chamber.

Jove!" shouted the little Englishman;
for in this bright thought there was yet
a ray of hope for them.

Tip-Top was agreeable. He felt perfectly safe, for he was sure that he stood
on firm conviction. His royal blood
was perhaps a little removed, but what
of that? he had never doubted for a
moment that he was a full-fledged
Tudor. Had he not heard his Aunt
Jane boast of it hundreds of times, and
did n't she always sign herself "Jane
Tudor Jenkins," and had n't the whole
family signed themselves Tudors for
generations past? So he walked up
very boldly, and laid his little open
book down by the broad page which
Pollyphrastus had before him, and
calmly awaited results.

Now, this Book of Wisdom was a
very curious book. It was a sort of
encyclopædia which furnished information upon any and all subjects of

interest to the Cerulites, and to the
Cerulites only.   It told them everything
they wanted to know, it proved everything they wanted to prove, and dis-
proved   everything   they   wanted   to
condemn;   and   they   believed   in   it   as
in an oracle.   It was the most obliging
and remarkable volume imaginable, and
its value, could not have been overes-
timated   by   the   Cerulites.   The   one
thing which it had not done, however,
was   to   tell   them   where   the   Rainbow
Valley was situated; and this was mys-
tifying.   But   there   was   a   reason   for
this.   This book had been compiled,
so   tradition   went,   by   an   inspired   Cerulite, who died very suddenly, — just as
he   was   preparing   to   begin   on   his
column of V's; and it was the com-
mon   belief   that   the   fairies   of   the
island, becoming jealous of his learning, and fearing lest he might divulge
their secret concerning the mysterious·

Valley, had taken him off rather un-
ceremoniously.

Pollyphrastus was the sole custodian
of this Book of Wisdom, and the only
person who knew all its ins and outs;
and he understood its mysterious work-
ings as well as he did his algebra. So
he immediately compared Tip-Top's
statement with that on the corresponding subject in the book before him.
And sure enough, there they were,
— the Jenkinses, the Joneses, the Sim-
monses, the Robinsons, — all branching
down to the trunk of the family-tree
with the most astonishing correctness
and precision, until it came to that
heedless person who had married her
sister's second cousin-in-law. Here, if
you please, matters took a sudden turn,
— melancholy enough for poor Tip-Top.
Pollyphrastus's countenance fell when
he came to that place. What could it
mean? The Book of Wisdom had never

played him such a trick. He read, in hollow tones, —

"And *she* married her sister's second cousin-in-law, and *he* was — was — was *not* a Tudor, — but a *Toodle!*"

"Impossible!" cried Tip-Top, his eyes as round as saucers. "There must be some mistake. It can't be that we — that I — that my Aunt Jane — that they have all been mistaken. Oh, please look again, do!"

He leaned over the page anxiously while Pollyphrastus pointed to the fatal words a second time; but there they were, in black and white, as plain as plain could be. That person's name was actually Toodle instead of Tudor; and the Book of Wisdom was infallible. Tip-Top was forced to resign himself to the inevitable.

"Well, I *am* surprised," was all he said, and tears of shame and disappointment stood in his pretty eyes.

Pollyphrastus reads from the Book of Wisdom.

It was certainly a most humiliating state of affairs, — to have thought one's self a Tudor all one's life, to have held one's head up for thinking one was a Tudor, to have aspired to the hand of a princess on the strength of one's being a Tudor, and then by a luckless accident to discover that one was only a Toodle, — a low-born Toodle! Tip-Top could not understand it. Doubtless some remote and uncultured great-aunt had pronounced Tudor Toodor, and afterwards Toodor had gradually become Toodle, and there lay all the trouble; but Tip-Top felt that he could never, never right himself in the eyes of all these aristocratic Cerulites.

The council broke up in an unusually solemn and gloomy manner. The victorious rivals did not dare show very much exultation over Tip-Top's discomfiture, for the king's face was a

sight to behold; and I think, too, that
in their inmost hearts they felt rather
sorry for poor little Tip-Top, who was
thus suddenly fallen into disrepute on
account of his Toodle ancestry. They
walked away, rather wondering what
would happen next. As for the princess Cerulea, she was carried away to
her bed-chamber, where, utterly regard-
less of consequences, she wept and
wailed just one hour and a quarter by
the clock.

III

THE RAINBOW VALLEY.

N the following morning the entire nation was apprised of the events just recorded. Nothing so nearly approaching a calamity had befallen the Cerulites since the days of that reckless young king who had fallen in love with and married the chimney-sweep's daughter. The royal family were steeped in a state of melancholy which, for them, amounted to despair. In vain did the councillors of state protest against the

7

indulgence of such dangerous senti-
ments on the part of their liege, and
endeavor to persuade him that things
were perhaps not as bad as they seemed,
and that it was always darkest before
the dawn; the king would not be com-
forted for the loss of such an eligible
son-in-law as Prince Tip-Top. All this
was felt in the atmosphere, and the
air was full of gossip and conjectures
about that little American impostor.
Tip-Top could bear it no longer; he
longed to get away and hide himself
from everybody. Sympathy was not
what he wanted just then; much less
could he face the revilings of his
enemies.

He started out to seek the quiet of
the woods and hills, choosing an unfre-
quented little path that led nobody
knew whither. He could think of
nothing but his late misfortune, and he
wanted to think of it alone, and perhaps,

after cool deliberation, find some way
out of it. It is needless to say that,
like all disappointed lovers, he had not
slept a wink the night before. He was
very miserable,—a state of mind which,
for political reasons, he felt obliged to
confide only to the trees and flowers
and the murmuring wavelets that came
lapping up against the shore. Everything was bright and warm and
summery. A soft haze rested on the
landscape. The birds floated lazily in
the air, and their songs came from out
the far distance as though they had
been singing in some other world. The
hills rose one after another like green
billows. The sea was blue with the
reflection of the cloudless sky, and the
fragrance of the budding trees filled the
whole air.

In the midst of this loveliness poor
little Tip-Top sighed, and he was very
wretched.

"Everything is happy," he thought, "everything is happy but me."

He walked on and on for hours, not knowing whither his steps were leading him, and not caring very much. He tried to think calmly, but it was a confusing business. Finally he gave way to his feelings.

"I wish I could lose myself," he said, misanthropically; "I wish I could lose myself so that they could never find me, and then perhaps *she* would care a little, and be sorry for me, and not believe that I am a real impostor, who tried to deceive them, when I never dreamed of such a thing as being a Toodle."

For if there were two things that hurt poor little Tip-Top's feelings more than anything else, it was having been called a "humbug" by those boasting rivals of his, and the thought that the Princess Cerulea might think him untruthful. You have no doubt guessed

that, by this time, he was very much in
love with the gentle Cerulea.   Indeed,
he thought he had never loved any one
so much.   This was partly because, as
matters stood then, there was no chance
whatever of his getting her, and partly
because she really was a very amiable
little person, in spite of her pale-blue
hair.   To tell the truth, Tip-Top had
actually grown to admire this more
than anything else about Cerulea.   It is
a curious thing enough, but you know
that when we love people very much,
even their little blemishes have a
certain charm for us.   Not that I
am dreaming of calling Cerulea's hair
a blemish, but Tip-Top himself had
thought it a little queer at first; and he
could hardly account for the strange
new feeling in him which made him
think that blue hair was the most desirable thing in the world.

   With all these feelings in his troubled

little heart, he still walked and walked without stopping. He seemed to be inspired, so to speak, to walk until he had walked off his melancholy. He felt he would soon come to a stopping-place, — what place, he did not know; but he felt sure that he heard voices in the whispering leaves all around him telling him which way to go.

He was not mistaken; for, as he came to a sudden turn in the road, he found himself in the midst of a beautiful little valley buried deep between two green hills. It looked so cool and quiet that he longed to stop and rest awhile under its inviting shades. There was a little spring bubbling out of the side of a rock, whose clear, colorless water ran out to fill a small lake near by. Tip-Top thought he had never seen any water look so tempting. He went up to it and drank several times out of the cup which he

made with his hand, for he had gone
a long way, and he was very warm
and thirsty. Then he spied a mossy
plot underneath a blossoming olive-tree,
with just a little patch of sky forming a
blue canopy above it. Tip-Top guessed
that this must be the couch of some
woodland nymph, and he began to
wonder if he had really stumbled into
fairy-land by accident. He had seen so
many strange things of late that this
seemed quite possible.

"As long as there seems to be no
one else here just now," he thought,
"I don't think it would be wrong for
me to lie down and rest awhile. I
am so tired, and I do want to forget
my trouble so. Perhaps a fairy will
come along after a while, and then I'll
ask her to help me make Princess
Cerulea forgive me for being a Toodle.
Good fairies always help people out
of their troubles; and I am sure only

good fairies can live in this beautiful place."

He stretched his tired little figure on the cool green moss, looked about him once or twice, and almost immediately his eyelids began to droop, and in a moment more Tip-Top was sound asleep in the mystic and unknown realms of the Rainbow Valley!

As soon as his eyes were closed, he began to dream the strangest, most delightful dream he had ever had. He thought that a perfect legion of fairies hovered over him, and smiled and talked, — not to him, but about him, — in the softest, silveriest voices that sounded like the whisperings of angels.

"What a dear little fellow!" said one of them.

"And what a nice good boy he is, too," said another. "Of course you know that he was in total ignorance about that vulgar-minded great-aunt of

Prince Tip-Top in trouble.

his, who so inconsequentially married a
Toodle instead of a Tudor."

"Of course; and what a disappointment it must have been to him!"

"And how sweetly he takes it," said
a third. "I'm sure it is a great pity;
for if any one deserves and ought to
win the princess, it is Prince Tip-Top."

Tip-Top was surprised to hear them
speak his name so familiarly, and wondered how they happened to know all
about him; but he soon remembered
that fairies know everything, — it is a
trick they have, you know.

"Not *Prince* Tip-Top any more, my
dear," said the second fairy, with rather
a sad smile.

"Yes, Prince Tip-Top he is, and
Prince Tip-Top he shall always be,"
insisted the first fairy. "See, the rainbow is just appearing in the sky above
his head. When he shall have slept
one hour under the blue light of the

rainbow, his hair will immediately turn to an exquisite shade of blue. Now, the royal family will never be able to resist it, for, after all, that is the truest indication of blue blood. Besides, Tip-Top is the only person who has ever walked to the end of the rainbow; I am sure that that is a distinction which ought to meet with great reward."

Thereupon all the fairies set up a chorus of joyful laughter that echoed and echoed down the green valley like the tinkling of distant bells; and not until it had died away completely did Tip-Top feel himself waking out of this happy and delicious sleep. When he opened his eyes the first thing he saw was the rainbow overhead, arching from one end of the little valley to the other, and flooding it with its varied lights.

"Oh, how beautiful everything is here!" he said, looking about him in astonishment. "It can't be possible —

"Prince Tip-Top he is, and Prince Tip-Top he shall always be."

it can't be true — that I have actually
found the Rainbow Valley, for which
the Cerulites have been looking for
more than a hundred years! I must
be dreaming."

But something seemed to tell him that
he was not dreaming. The wind that
rustled among the leaves said plainly,
" This is the Rainbow Valley ; " the
birds that flew in and out of the branches
looked at him oddly, and seemed to be
saying, " Lucky boy! you have found
the Rainbow Valley ; " the little spring
murmured the same thing as it trickled
down the rocks and pebbles ; and Tip-
Top was overjoyed. He picked up his
cap and ran to the spring.

"Oh, little spring," he cried, " I am
so glad! and I thank you so much for
letting me find you!" and he drank
once more of its pure cold water.
Then he looked in the lake, and saw
the blue and pink and yellow rainbow

reflected on its clear surface, and he
saw, too, his own image as clearly as
in a looking-glass,—his pretty, rosy face
and eager eyes, his slender, graceful
figure, and his curls, changed to a hue
surpassing even Cerulea's lovely hair.

"Oh, oh!" he cried aloud, "I look
like somebody else; I don't look one
bit like myself. What is the matter
with my hair?" and for a minute he did
not know whether to be glad or sorry.

"Oh, dear! this is very singular," he
kept repeating to himself. "What will
my Aunt Jane think; and won't the
boys at home shout when they see
me?" and he twirled one of his pretty
curls about his finger with a half-
amused, half-regretful look.

To be sure, he had admired blue hair
exceedingly only an hour before, and he
did think that blue hair was charming
for ladies, — strictly for ladies; but
when it came to losing his own pretty

yellow curls, he felt that he should like
to draw the line there; for he could not
help thinking of the mortification it
would cause his fastidious Aunt Jane to
see him in this ridiculous plight.

Just then a saucy little humming-bird
flew up and alighted on his shoulder,
looked straight at him in the most
intrepid manner, and laughed outright,
— that is, as well as a humming-bird
can laugh, — in a way that said as
plainly as words, —

"Why, you ignorant little goose,
don't you know that the fairies will
make that all right? Just at present
you are in the height of the style. So
don't worry about what your Aunt
Jane will say, but go and show yourself
to the king and queen, tell them you
have just discovered the Rainbow
Valley, and hear what *they* say!
And don't forget to be grateful for
your blessings!"

8

Tip-Top felt better at once. He turned and excused himself to the humming-bird, just as if he had been talking to a real person.

" I hope you won't think me ungrateful," said he; "indeed, I am very, very thankful for all I have seen in this beautiful valley to-day. But I 'm not quite myself yet. It makes a fellow feel a little queer to have his hair change color so suddenly, just at first, you understand. I 've no doubt I shall get used to it. If you have no objection, I think I had better hurry back, as it must be getting late. To-morrow I 'll go and show myself to the royal family, and surprise everybody."

The humming-bird winked approvingly and flew away, and Tip-Top bade farewell to the Rainbow Valley and was off.

He found his way back as easily as he had come, and it did not take him nearly as long, for his heart and his heels were light, and he tripped along as if he had been on wings. In a very short time he was in sight of the king's palace. Before nearing the public thoroughfares, however, he carefully tucked all his curls inside his cap, so as not to call attention to his change of appearance, because he wanted to surprise the king, the queen, and the Princess Cerulea first of all.

When he reached the city everybody seemed to be in the same happy frame of mind which he enjoyed: the bells were ringing, the trumpets were blowing, the flags were hoisted, the Cerulites were all out, rushing around in a frantic sort of way. Tip-Top felt sure it must be the setting in of the reaction of yesterday's calamity. He walked a little faster through the crowd, not stopping to ask any questions. But at the gate of the palace he was met by the master

of ceremonies, who appeared to be in
an hilarious and playful mood.

"What's all this?" inquired Tip-
Top.

"Bless your sweet worship, Mr. Tip-
Top, have n't you heard?"

"Heard what?" asked Tip-Top, in
some curiosity.

"Why, of the king's turnamint? It's
the greatest thing that ever was in this
benighted land," said the master of
ceremonies, with a touch of sarcasm.
"It's all that French young gentleman's
doings, too. He would n't rest till they
had a turnamint. He said turnamints
was the most aristocratic things in the
world. Kings always had them when
they wanted to settle an important
question. So a turnamint it is; and all
Miss Cerulea's noble suitors is just
a spreading of themselves this very
minute, and the one that cuts up the
biggest antic is going to win her for his

bride. Why is n't your lordship there? They are all waiting for you."

Tip-Top started at this piece of information.

"Well, I never!" he exclaimed; and made his way to the palace without further parley with the genial servant.

The truth of the matter was that Princess Cerulea felt it her duty to accept a husband from among her foreign admirers, though she did not care a straw for any of them, except Tip-Top. Yet she could not be induced to make a choice. So when the little French nobleman proposed a contest as a means of settling the matter, she joyfully accepted the plan, hoping that Tip-Top would hear of it and would, for her sake, distinguish himself in a way that would distance all his rivals. Instead of that, Tip-Top had been napping in the Rainbow Valley, and devoting himself to fairies and the like all day!

But for a little boy Tip-Top was a good deal of a diplomat. He resolved to lose no more time, and turning the matter carefully in his mind as he went to his room, he determined to break the news of his discovery to the assembled Cerulites with the most highly dramatic effect.

Sure enough, a grand tournament was being held at the palace. All the dignitaries of the land were present, — the king and queen and the Princess Cerulea occupying, of course, the most prominent seats; near them sat the estimable Pollyphrastus, who was to make the decision ; and behind him were the lords chamberlain and the maids of honor, with all their relations, — in fact, everybody whose good opinion was of any account whatsoever was present. All sat there in expectation of the remarkable feats of the young heroes. The suitors stood up in a row in their gayest and most festive costumes. They were all there but Tip-Top, — a fact which gave rise to some comment on the part of those who were interested in his success, and to considerable tremor in the bosom of the gentle Cerulea.

Young Bourbon, who was eager for the fray, suggested that doubtless Monsieur Tip-Top had had the grace to withdraw from the contest on account of his base origin and out of compliment to his betters. You may be sure that this audacious French young person was silenced without much ceremony by the lord high executioner, who was a rank Tip-Topite. But after many preliminaries had been gone through with, and vain inquiries made after the missing suitor by his friends, and divers manifestations of impatience exhibited on the part of the competitors, the " lists were opened," so to speak, and the contest began.

The first to appear was the little
Esquimaux, who perhaps you remember,
and who performed a remarkable bear-
dance all by himself, to the great delight

of all the little Okusheeans. His *début*
before such a critical audience was considered a great success, and he was
encored and encored in a way that
was very flattering to his hopes; even
Cerulea condescended to smile her ap-

proval of him. And he was so elated
that he appeared and re-appeared, and
danced and danced, till his little legs
were nearly danced off, and he had to
to be dragged away by the assistants of
the lord high executioner.

The entertainment proceeded, and
the delectable heir of the royal house of
Rothnase made his appearance. He
began by delivering a long speech,
which, being in German, unfortunately
no one understood; but it sounded very
grand. Then, by the most dexterous
acrobatic feat he suddenly turned a
somersault and landed on his head. In
this precarious attitude he drank, without the slightest hesitation, one, two,
three, five, nay, ten, glasses of beer!
The Cerulites began to open their eyes.
Here was truly an exceedingly well-
balanced young person. He drank
twelve glasses, and shouts and hand-
kerchiefs went up on all sides. He

drank one more glass, and the house fairly reeled with applause. But alas! even glory must have its end. By the most natural process in the world those thirteen glasses of beer went to the illustrious Rothnase's head, and in a moment more *he* had to be carried away for repairs.

Young Bourbon next came to the front, with an air of high-bred *abandon*, and a supercilious expression of countenance which said, as plain as might be, "How simple those poor fellows are, and how trivial their feats. Now, kind friends, observe me, and see them pale into insignificance!"

He made a bow, threw up his arms, and forthwith executed a series of "cartwheels" that fairly captured the house. His little arms and legs were something startling to witness as they whirled by with the rapidity of a windmill; and when he had been before his audience three times in succession, he retired with a great flourish, albeit with something of a dizzy feeling in his aristocratic little head.

The next champion was the Turkish pasha, who came forward smoking a long hookah, and who did nothing worth mentioning, but strutted about trying to look bewitching, for the benefit of the ladies, and failing signally. At length he gathered up his ample trousers and tried to run a race with himself, in which effort his pipe came out a-head; and he made such a simpleton of himself that he was finally laughed out of the lists with ignominy.

As for the knight of the Star and Garter, it pains me to state that he had eaten so much roast beef at dinner that he fell fast asleep during the performance, and not hearing his name when it was called out, completely let his turn go by. I do not know just in what man-

ner he meant to distinguish himself, but
I have no doubt it was a great disappointment to him to be thus ruled
out through his own sleepiness and

carelessness. He was not missed, either,
which was a still more bitter vexation
to him, for almost immediately the little
Chinaman stepped up to greet the
eager public.

Now, his Excellency the worthy

Prince Sum-Fun had taken a cold in
his noble head, so that partly for this
reason, and partly from nervousness
and embarrassment at finding himself
confronted by so many great personages, he began to sneeze in a most
uproarious and unseemly fashion. The
little Cerulites applauded him with
genuine enthusiasm, and the more they
clapped the more he sneezed. The
king and queen were enchanted. Princess Cerulea declared she had never
heard such melodious and artistic
sneezing in all her life; and sneezing
bade fair to become the most fashionable accomplishment of the day. But
you have all heard of vaulting ambition
that o'erleaped itself and fell on the
other side. Well, Prince Sum-Fun
waxed so enthusiastic over his success, and sneezed so long and so
vociferously that he finally succeeded
in sneezing off his beautiful pig-tail.

At this unexpected feat the crowd
shouted with laughter, and there really
seemed nothing more to be desired in
the way of achievements. There were
still a number of young suitors who
were waiting their turns; but these
were passed by without notice, — which
caused them to smile a very blue sort
of smile at the irony of their fate.
Pollyphrastus wanted to decide in favor
of Prince Sum-Fun without any further
ado, when — thanks to Cerulea's lucky
star! — a herald rushed into the midst
of the agitated multitude, and blew a
sounding blast on his trumpet.

"Halt! attention!" he cried out,
as soon as the noise had subsided.
"There is still one more competitor,
and one who must be heard!"

Everybody waited in breathless expectation, and Princess Cerulea's heart
began to beat violently. Away down
the long line of spectators there

appeared suddenly a little figure in
a bewildering costume of white and
gold and a dainty feathered cap, and
lovely soft blue ringlets falling about
his shoulders; and in a twinkling every
one had recognized Prince Tip-Top.

He walked up in his most graceful
and engaging manner, and knelt on one
knee before the king and queen, and
looked up with a bright, happy smile at
Cerulea, who, in turn, threw down a
flower, which he picked up and placed
in his button-hole. He did not speak
for a while, — indeed, he could not have
been heard if he had spoken, so wild
were the people with excitement, and
so great was the commotion. Besides,
there was very little need for explana-
tion. The marvellous transformation
in his hair spoke for itself. Everybody
guessed, naturally, that Tip-Top had
made the great discovery, and had
taken advantage of it to enhance his

own sweet looks.   Finally, when the
king had quieted the frantic multitude,
Tip-Top stood up, and said, in his most
gracious and winning voice, —

"Ladies and gentlemen, — I mean,
My lords and ladies, — quite by accident, yesterday, I stumbled into the
Rainbow Valley, and you now behold
the result!   I shall be very glad to
show you all the way to this beautiful
place," and he made a magnificent ges-
ture with his hand, that generously took
in all his rivals; "but, of course, I
expect to have my reward, as I was the
first one to find it; and the only reward
I ask is the hand of the Princess
Cerulea."   Then he made a low bow,
and looked so pretty, and yet so manly,
that immediately the king and queen
flew down and embraced him: whereupon Cerulea followed their example,
and the matter was settled then and
there, to the great joy of the Cerulites,

Princess Cerulea throws a flower to Prince Tip-Top.

and Princess Cerulea became Princess
Tip-Top forever after.

As for the other suitors, the brilliant
heroes of but a few minutes before, it
was now their turn to feel a little blue.
Some of them said they felt as insig-
nificant as crawling bugs, and wished
they had never been born. It seemed
incredible that this slip of a boy, with
his rosy face and pretty smiles, should
actually have outdone them all, in spite
of his Toodle origin. This was such
a shock to their sensitive natures that
they vowed they should never get over
it; but of course they did.

Prince Tip-Top was promoted to the
highest dignities in Okushee, as the
discoverer of the long-sought Rainbow
Valley, and the Cerulites held long and
protracted festivities in honor of the
happy event. And after that, all persons who wished to make themselves
still more aristocratic and beautiful,

went and slept for one hour in the
Rainbow Valley, and came away a joy
to all their friends.

And of course, in due time, Prince
Tip-Top and the fair Cerulea were
married, and the wedding was the most
gorgeous affair in all the history of
Okushee. The gayeties lasted five
whole days, and the foreign princes,
who had determined to start for their
respective homes on the very day of
their discomfiture, were finally prevailed
upon to stay over for the ceremony;
and they declared afterwards that they
had never witnessed so regal or so en-
joyable a wedding. And they all went
home in good spirits, all excepting poor
little Sum-Fun, who remained inconsol-
able for the loss of his beauty.

Then Prince Tip-Top and his lovely
bride sailed away on their wedding
journey in a beautiful little barge
draped in silk and purple, and manned

by fifty of Okushee's most skilful oars-
men. And as it glided out into the
blue sea, straightway a lovely rainbow
stretched across the heavens above
them and shot a golden streak athwart
the water, and when they passed in
this golden ray of rainbow, immediately
Tip-Top's own beautiful curls assumed
their natural golden hue, and those of
his little bride became of the same
color, and indeed the whole of the airy
ship was for a moment transformed
into a golden boat by the light that
fell upon it.

Then a great deal of shouting and
waving of hands went up from the
shore where the royal couple and all
the great Cerulitic dignitaries had come
to see the happy pair off, while Tip-
Top and Cerulea stood hand in hand
at the stern, bowing and smiling their
farewell.

I am not sure whether Prince Tip-.

Top ever returned to his own country to tell his wonderful adventures to his Aunt Jane, or to show her and the boys his lovely little bride, or whether he preferred to spend the remainder of his life in the land of the Cerulites, and to be young and light-hearted always. But I do know that wherever he went he made sunshine around him, that he helped people out of their troubles by his cleverness and kind heart, and that, like all the other lovers in the Land of Impossibility, he and his little princess were happy and gay forever and a day.

THE END.